I0634366

John Godfrey Saxe

Clever Stories of many Nations

John Godfrey Saxe

Clever Stories of many Nations

ISBN/EAN: 9783743305724

Manufactured in Europe, USA, Canada, Australia, Japa

Cover: Foto ©Andreas Hilbeck / pixelio.de

Manufactured and distributed by brebook publishing software
(www.brebook.com)

John Godfrey Saxe

Clever Stories of many Nations

CLEVER STORIES

of

MANY NATIONS,

RENDERED in RHYME.

By

JOHN G. SAXE.

BOSTON
TICKNOR AND FIELDS
1865

CLEVER STORIES

OF

MANY NATIONS.

RENDERED IN RHYME BY

John G. Saxe.

ILLUSTRATED BY W. L. CHAMPNEY.

BOSTON:
TICKNOR AND FIELDS.
1865.

CONTENTS.

THE TREASURE OF GOLD.

A LEGEND OF ITALY.

THE TREASURE OF GOLD.

A LEGEND OF ITALY.

I.

 BEAUTIFUL story, my darlings,
    Though exceedingly quaint and old,
Is a tale I have read in Italian,
    Entitled, The Treasure of Gold.

II.

There lived near the town of Bologna
 A widow of virtuous fame, .
Alone with her only daughter, —
 Madonna LUCREZIA by name.

III.

A lady whom changing fortune
 Had numbered among the poor ;
And she kept an inn by the wayside,
 For the use of peasant and boor.

IV.

One day at the door of the tavern
 Three roving banditti appeared,
And one was a wily Venetian,
 To guess by his curious beard.

V.

And he spoke to the waiting hostess
 In phrases exceedingly fine,
And sat himself down with his fellows,
 And called for a flagon of wine.

VI.

At length, after deeply discoursing
  In voices suspiciously low,
The travellers rose from the table,
  And made preparation to go.

VII.

" Madonna," up spoke the Venetian,
  " Pray do us the kindness to hold
Awhile, for our better convenience,
  This snug little treasure of gold."

VIII.

" Indeed," said the smiling Lucrezia,
  " You 're welcome to leave it, — but stay ;
I have never a lock in my hovel,
  And the bag may, be stolen away.

IX.

" Besides," said the woman, " consider
  There 's no one the fact to attest ;
In pledge for so precious a treasure
  You have only my word, at the best."

X.

"In faith!" said the civil Venetian,
  "We have n't a morsel of fear;
But to guard against awkward mischances,
  Let the matter in writing appear."

XI.

And this was a part of the writing
  She gave the banditti to hold: —
"Not to one, nor to two, but to all,
  Will I render the treasure of gold."

XII.

Now the robbers were scarcely departed,
  When the cunning Venetian came back,
With, "Madam, allow me the favor
  Of putting my seal to the sack."

XIII.

But the moment she gave him the treasure,
  A horseman rode up, — and behold!
While the woman went out to attend him,
  The villain ran off with the gold.

XIV.

" Alas !" cried the widow, in anguish,
  " Alas for my daughter forlorn !
I would we had perished together,
  The day GIANNETTA was born !"

XV.

In sooth, she had reason for sorrow,
  Although it were idle to weep ;
She was sued in the court of Bologna,
  For the money she promised to keep.

XVI.

" Now go, GIANNETTA," she faltered,
  " To one that is versed in the laws ;
But stop at the shrine of the Virgin,
  And beg her to favor our cause."

XVII.

Alas for Madonna LUCREZIA !
  In vain GIANNETTA applied
To each lawyer of note in the city ;
  They were all on the opposite side.

XVIII.

At last, as the sorrowing maiden
  Sat pondering her misery over,
And breathing a prayer to the Virgin,
  She thought of Lorenzo, her lover;

XIX.

A student well read in the statutes,
  According to common report,
But one who, from modest aversion,
  Had never appeared in the court.

XX.

" I 'll try ! " said the faithful LORENZO,
  After hearing her narrative through ;
" And for strength in the hour of trial,
  I 'll think, GIANNETTA, of you ! "

XXI.

Next morning the judges assembled ;
  The claimants' attorneys were heard,
And gave a most plausible version
  Of how the transaction occurred ;

XXII.

Then showed, by the widow's confession,
    She had taken the money to hold,
And proved that, though often requested,
    She failed to surrender the gold.

XXIII.

The judges seemed fairly impatient
    To utter the fatal decree,
When lo! the young student Lorenzo
    Stands up, and commences a plea: —

XXIV.

" Your Honors : — I speak for the widow ;
    Some words have been (carelessly) said
Concerning a written agreement, —
    I ask that the writing be read."

XXV.

" Of course," said the Court, " it is proper
    The writing appear in the case ;
The sense of a written agreement
    May give it a different face."

XXVI.

" Observe," said the student, " the bargain, —
　　To which we are willing to hold, —
' *Not to one, nor to two, but to all*,
　　Will I render the treasure of gold.'

XXVII.

" We stand by the writing, your Honors,
　　And candidly ask of you whether
These fellows can sue for their money
　　Till they come and demand it together ? "

XXVIII.

And so it was presently settled,
　　For so did the judges decide ;
And great was the joy of the widow,
　　And great was her daughter's pride.

XXIX.

And fast grew the fame of LORENZO,
　　For making so clever a plea,
Till never in all Bologna
　　Was lawyer so wealthy as he !

XXX.

And he married his own GIANNETTA,
  As the story is pleasingly told, —
And such were the bane and the blessing
  That came of the Treasure of Gold!

THE NOBLEMAN, THE FISHER-
MAN, AND THE PORTER.

THE NOBLEMAN, THE FISHERMAN, AND THE PORTER.

A LEGEND OF ITALY.

I.

T was a famous nobleman
    Who flourished in the East,
  And once upon a holiday
He made a goodly feast,
And summoned in of kith and kin
  A hundred at the least.

II.

Now while they sat in social chat
  Discoursing frank and free,
In came the steward, with a bow :
  " A man below," said he,
" Has got, my lord, the finest fish
  That ever swam the sea ! "

III.

" Indeed ! " exclaimed the nobleman,
  " Then buy it in a trice ;
The finest fish that ever swam
  Must needs be very nice ;
Go, buy it of the fisherman,
  And never mind the price."

IV.

" And so I would," the steward said,
  " But, faith, he would n't hear
A word of money for his fish,
  (Was ever man so queer ?)
But said he thought a hundred stripes
  Could not be counted dear."

V.

"Go bring him here," my lord replied ;
　"The man I fain would see ;
A merry wag, by your report,
　This fisherman must be ! "
"Go bring him here !　Go bring him here ! "
　Cried all the company.

VI.

The steward did as he was bid,
　When thus my lord began :
"For this fine fish what may you wish ?
　I'll buy it, if I can."
"One hundred lashes on my back !"
　Exclaimed the fisherman.

VII.

"Now, by the rood ! but this is good,"
　The laughing lord replied ;
"Well, let the fellow have his way ;
　Go, call a groom ! " he cried ;
"But let the payment he demands
　Be modestly applied."

VIII.

He bared his back and took the lash
　　As it were merry play ;
But at the fiftieth stroke, he said,
　　"Good master groom, I pray
Desist a moment, if you please ;
　　I have a word to say.

IX.

I have a partner in the case, —
　　The fellow standing there ;
Pray take the jacket off his back,
　　And let him have his share ;
That one of us should take the whole
　　Were surely hardly fair !"

X.

"A partner ? " cried the nobleman,
　　"Who can the fellow mean ? "
"I mean," replied the fisherman,
　　With countenance serene,
" *Your porter there !* — the biggest knave
　　That ever yet was seen !

XI.

" The rogue who stopped me at the gate,
   And would n't let me in
Until I swore to give him half
   Of all my fish should win.
I 've got my share ! Pray let, my lord,
   His payment now begin ! "

XII.

" What you propose," my lord replied,
   " Is nothing more than fair ;
Here, groom, — lay on a hundred stripes,
   And mind you do not spare ;
The scurvy dog shall never say
   He did n't get his share ! "

XIII.

Then all that goodly company,
   They laughed with might and main,
The while beneath the stinging lash
   The porter writhed in pain.
" So fare all villains," quoth my lord,
   " Who seek dishonest gain ! "

XIV.

Then turning to the fisherman,
　　Who still was standing near,
He filled his hand with golden coins,
　　Some twenty sequins clear,
And bade him come and take the like
　　On each succeeding year.

ALWAYS IN LUCK;

OR,

THE SEER IN SPITE OF HIMSELF.

AN ARABIAN TALE.

ALWAYS IN LUCK.

AN ARABIAN TALE.

I.

IN Cairo once there dwelt a worthy man,
    Toilsome and frugal, but extremely poor;
"Howe'er," he grumbled, "I may toil and plan,
The wolf is ever howling at my door,
While arrant rascals thrive and prosper: hence
I much misdoubt the ways of Providence.

II.

"Allah is Allah ; and, we all agree,
  Mohammed is his Prophet.   Be it so ;
But what 's Mohammed ever done for me,
  To boil my kettle I should like to know ?
The thieves fare better, — and I much incline
From this day forth to make their calling mine."

III.

"Dog of an Arab !" cried his pious spouse,
  "So you would steal to better your estate,
And hasten Allah's vengeance !   Shame ! arouse !
  Why sit you there repining at your fate ?
Pray to the Prophet, sinner that you are,
Then wash your face and go to the Bazaar.

IV.

"Take with you pen and paper and a book,
  And, sitting in a corner, gravely make
Some mystic scrawls, — put on a solemn look,
  As if you were a wise and learned sheik ;
And, mark my word, the people in a trice
Will come in throngs to purchase your advice."

V.

" 'T is worth a trial, woman, I confess ;
   Things can't be worse," the moody Arab said ;
" But then, alas ! I have no proper dress,
   Not e'en a turban to adorn my head."
"Allah be praised !" — just here the woman spied
A hollow pumpkin lying at her side.

VI.

" See, this will do !" and, cutting it in twain,
   She placed the half upon her husband's pate :
" 'T is quaint and grave, and well befits thy brain,
   Most reverend master," cried the dame, elate :
" Now to thy labor hasten thee away,
And thou shalt prosper from this very day !"

VII.

And so, obedient to his wife's command,
   The anxious sheik procured a little nook
In the Bazaar, where, sitting by a stand,
   With much grimace he pored upon his book,
Peering around, at intervals, to spy
A customer, if such a thing were nigh.

VIII.

And soon, indeed, a customer appeared,
  A peasant pale and sweating with distress ;
" Good Father Pumpkin ! may your mighty beard "
  (Bowing in reverence) " be never less !
I come to crave your counsel, — for, alas !
Most learned Father, I have lost my ass."

IX.

" Now, curse the donkey ! " cried the puzzled man
  (Unto himself), " and curse Fatima, too,
Who sent me here ! — for, do the best I can,
  And that 's the best that any one can do,
I 'm sure to blunder."   So, in sheer despair,
He named the graveyard : " Seek your donkey there ! "

X.

It chanced the ass that very moment grazed
  Within the graveyard, as the sheik had told ;
And so the peasant, joyful and amazed,
  Gave thanks and money ; nor could he withhold
His pious prayers, but, bowing to the ground,
Cried : " Great is Allah ! for my ass is found ! "

XI.

" Allah *is* Allah!" said the grateful sheik,
  Returning homeward with his precious fee ;
" I much rejoice for dear Fatima's sake ;
  Few men, in sooth, have such a mate as she ;
Most wives are bosh, or worse than bosh, but mine
In wit and beauty is almost divine ! "

XII.

Next day he hastened early to his post,
  But found some clients had arrived before ;
One eager dame a skein of silk had lost ;
  Another money ; and a dozen more,
Of either sex, were waiting to recover
A fickle mistress or a truant lover.

XIII.

With solemn face the sheik replied to each,
  Whate'er his whim might move his tongue to say ;
And all turned out according to his speech ;
  And so it chanced for many a lucky day,
Till " Father Pumpkin " grew a famous seer,
Whose praise had even reached the Sultan's ear.

XIV.

"Allah is Allah!" cried the happy sheik,
  "And never more, Fatima, will I doubt
Mohammed is his prophet; let us take
  Our ease henceforward —" Here a sudden shout
Announced the Sultan's janissaries, sent,
They said, to seize him, but with kind intent.

XV.

"The Grand Seraglio has been robbed by knaves
  Of all the royal jewels; and the Porte,
To get them back again, your presence craves
  In Stamboul; he will pay you richly for 't,
If you succeed; if not, why then, instead
Of getting money — you will lose your head!"

XVI.

"My curse upon thee!" cried the angry man
  Unto Fatima; "see what thou hast done!
O woman, woman! Since the world began,
  All direst mischiefs underneath the sun
Are woman's doing —" Here the Sultan's throng
Of janissaries bade him, "Come along!"

XVII.

The Seer's arival being now proclaimed
  Throughout the capital, the robbers quake
With very fear ; while, trembling and ashamed,
  In deeper terror sits the wretched sheik,
Cursing Fatima for a wicked wife,
Whose rash ambition has betrayed his life.

XVIII.

" But seven short days my sands have yet to run,
  And then, alas ! I lose my foolish head ;
These seven white beans I 'll swallow, one by one,
  To mark each passing day ere I am dead.
Alas ! alas ! the Sultan's hard decree !
The sun is setting : *there goes one !* " said he.

XIX.

Just then a thief (the leader of the band
  Who stole the Sultan's jewels), passing by,
Heard the remark, and saw the lifted hand,
  And ran away as fast as he could fly,
To tell his comrades that, beyond a doubt,
The cunning seer had fairly found them out.

XX.

Next day another, ere the hour was dark,
    Passed by the casement where the sheik was seen;
His hand was lifted warningly, and hark!
    "*There goes a second!*" (swallowing the bean).
The robber fled, amazed, and told the crew
'T was time to counsel what were best to do!

XXI.

But still, — as if the faintest doubt to cure, —
    The following eve the robbers sent a third;
And so till six had made the matter sure,
    (For unto each the same event occurred,)
When, taking counsel, they at once agreed
To seek the wizard and confess the deed.

XXII.

"Most reverend father!" thus the chief began,
    "Thy thoughts are just; thy spoken words are true;
To hide from thee surpasses mortal man;
    Our evil works henceforward we eschew,
For now we know that sinning never thrives:
Here, take the jewels, but O spare our lives!"

XXIII.

" The law enjoins," the joyful sheik replied,

   " That bloody Death shall end the robber's days ;

But, that your sudden virtue may be tried,

   Swear on the Koran you will mend your ways,

And then depart."   The robbers roundly swore,

In Allah's name, that they would rob no more.

XXIV.

" Allah *is* Allah ! " cried the grateful sheik,

   Holding the jewels in the vizier's face.

The vizier answered, " Sir, be pleased to take

   The casket to the Sultan."   " No, your Grace,"

The sheik replied : " the gems are *here*, you see ;

Pray, tell the Sultan he may come to me ! "

XXV.

The Sultan came, and, ravished to behold

   The precious jewels to his hand restored,

He made the finder rich in thanks and gold,

   And on the instant pledged his royal word,

And straight confirmed it in the Prophet's name,

To grant whatever he might choose to claim !

XXVI.

"Sire of the Faithful! publish a decree,"
   The sheik made answer, "and proclaim to all,
That none henceforth shall ever question me
   Of any matter either great or small;
I ask no more.   So shall my labors cease;
My waning life I fain would spend in peace."

XXVII.

The Sultan answered: "Be it even so;
   And may your beard increase a thousand fold;
And may your house with children overflow!"
   And so the sheik, o'erwhelmed with praise and gold,
Returned unto the city whence he came,
Blessing Mohammed's and Fatima's name!

THE KING AND THE COTTAGER.

A PERSIAN TALE.

THE KING AND THE COTTAGER.

A PERSIAN TALE.

I.

PRAY list unto a legend
    The ancient poets tell;
'T is of a mighty monarch
    In Persia once did dwell;
A mighty queer old monarch,
    Who ruled his kingdom well.

II.

" I must build another palace,"
    Observed this mighty king ;
" For this is getting shabby
    Along the southern wing ;
And, really, for a monarch,
    It is n't quite the thing !

III.

" So I will have a new one,
    Although I greatly fear
To build it just to suit me
    Will cost me rather dear ;
And I 'll choose, God wot, another spot
    Much finer than this here ! "

IV.

So he travelled o'er his kingdom
    A proper site to find,
Where he might build a palace
    Exactly to his mind,
All with a pleasant prospect
    Before it and behind.

V.

Not far with this endeavor
  The king had travelled round,
Ere, to his royal pleasure,
  A charming spot he found ;
But an ancient widow's hovel
  Was standing on the ground.

VI.

" Ah ! here," exclaimed the monarch,
  " Is just the proper spot,
If this woman would allow me
  To remove her little cot " ;
But the beldam answered plainly,
  She 'd rather he would not !

VII.

" Within this lowly cottage,
  Great monarch, I was born ;
And only from this cottage
  By Death will I be torn ;
So spare it, in your justice,
  Or spoil it, in your scorn ! "

VIII.

Then all the courtiers mocked her
  With cruel words and jeers :
"'T is plain her royal master
  She neither loves nor fears ;
We would knock her ugly hovel
  About her ugly ears !

IX.

" When ever was a subject
  Who might the king withstand ?
Or deem his spoken pleasure
  As less than his command ?
Of course he 'll rout the beldam,
  And confiscate her land ! "

X.

But, to their deep amazement,
  His Majesty replied :
" Good woman, never heed them,
  The *king* is on your side ;
Your cottage is your castle,
  And here you shall abide !

XI.

" To raze it in a moment
  The power is mine, I grant ;
My absolute dominion
  A hundred poets chant, —
For being *Khan* of Persia,
  There 's nothing that I *can't !* "

XII.

('T was in this pleasant fashion
  The gracious monarch spoke ;
For kings have merry fancies,
  Like other mortal folk ;
And none so high and mighty
  But loves his little joke.)

XIII.

" But power is scarcely worthy
  Of honor or applause,
That in its domination
  Contemns the widow's cause,
Or perpetrates injustice
  By trampling on the laws.

XIV.

"That I have wronged the weakest,
    No honest tongue may say ;
So bide you in your cottage,
    Good woman, while you may ;
What 's yours by deed and purchase,
    No man may take away !

XV.

"And I will build beside it ;
    For though your cot may be
In such a goodly presence
    No fitting thing to see,
If it honor not my castle,
    It will surely honor me !

XVI.

"For so my loyal people
    Who gaze upon the sight
Shall know that in oppression
    I do not take delight,
Nor hold a king's convenience
    Before a subject's right !"

XVII.

Now from his spoken purpose
   The king departed not ;
He built the royal dwelling
   Upon the chosen spot ;
And there they stood together,
   The palace and the cot !

XVIII.

Sure such unseemly neighbors
   Were never seen before ;
" His Majesty is doting ! "
   Some silly courtiers swore ;
But all true loyal subjects,
   They loved the king the more.

XIX.

Long, long he ruled his kingdom
   In honor and renown ;
But danger ever threatens
   The head that wears a crown ;
And Fortune, tired of smiling,
   For once put on a frown.

XX.

For ever secret envy
    Attends a high estate ;
And ever lurking malice
    Pursues the good and great ;
And ever base ambition
    Will end in deadly hate.

XXI.

And so two wicked courtiers,
    Who long had strove in vain,
By craft and evil counsels,
    To mar the monarch's reign,
Contrived a scheme infernal
    Whereby he should be slain.

XXII.

But, as all deeds of darkness
    Are wont to leave a clew
Before the glaring sunlight
    To bring the knaves to view,
That sin may be rewarded,
    And Satan get his due, —

XXIII.

To plan their wicked treason
  They sought a lonely spot
Behind the royal palace,
  Hard by the widow's cot,
Who heard their machinations,
  And straight revealed the plot !

XXIV.

" I see," exclaimed the Persian,
  " The just are wise alone ;
Who spares the rights of others
  May chance to guard his own ;
The widow's humble cottage
  Has propped a monarch's throne ! "

THE TARTAR WHO CAUGHT A TARTAR.

A HUNGARIAN LEGEND.

THE TARTAR WHO CAUGHT A TARTAR.

A HUNGARIAN LEGEND.

I.

HERE 'S trouble in Hungary, now, alas!
  There 's trouble on every hand ;
    For that terrible man,
    The Tartar Khan,
  Is ravaging over the land !

II.

He is riding forth with his ugly men,
To rob and ravish and slay :
    For deeds like those,
    You may well suppose,
Are quite in the Tartar-way.

III.

And now he comes, that terrible chief,
To a mansion grand and old :
    And he peers about
    Within and without,
And what do his eyes behold ?

IV.

A thousand cattle in fold and field,
And sheep all over the plain,
    And noble steeds,
    Of rarest breeds,
And beautiful crops of grain.

V.

But finer still is the hoarded wealth
That his ravished eyes behold,
    In silver plate
    Of wondrous weight,
And jewels of pearl and gold!

VI.

A nobleman owns this fine estate :
And when the robber he sees,
    'T is not very queer
    He quakes with fear,
And trembles a bit in the knees!

VII.

He quakes in fear of his precious life,
And scarce suppressing a groan,
    " Good Tartar," says he,
    " Whatever you see
Be pleased to reckon your own ! "

VIII.

The Khan looked round in a leisurely way
As one who is puzzled to choose ;
    When, cocking his ear,
    He chanced to hear
The creak of feminine shoes !

IX.

The Tartar smiled a villanous smile,
When, like a lily in bloom,
    A lady fair
    With golden hair
Came gliding into the room !

X.

The robber stared with amorous eyes ;
Was ever so winning a face ?
    And long he gazed
    As one amazed
To see such beauty and grace !

XI.

A moment more, and the lawless man
Had seized his struggling prey,
    Without remorse,
    And — taking horse —
He bore the lady away!

XII.

" Now Heaven be praised!" the nobleman cried,
" For many a mercy to me!
    I bow me still
    Unto His will.
God pity the Tartar!" said he.

THE BLIND MEN AND THE ELEPHANT.

A HINDOO FABLE.

THE BLIND MEN AND THE ELEPHANT.

A HINDOO FABLE.

I.

T was six men of Indostan,
　　To learning much inclined,
　　Who went to see the Elephant,
　（Though all of them were blind,)
　That each by observation
　　Might satisfy his mind.

II.

The *First* approached the Elephant,
  And happening to fall
Against his broad and sturdy side,
  At once began to bawl:
" God bless me! — but the Elephant
  Is very like a wall!"

III.

The *Second*, feeling of the tusk,
  Cried, " Ho! what have we here
So very round and smooth and sharp?
  To me 't is mighty clear
This wonder of an Elephant
  Is very like a spear!"

IV.

The *Third* approached the animal,
  And, happening to take
The squirming trunk within his hands,
  Thus boldly up and spake: —
" I see," quoth he, " the Elephant
  Is very like a snake!"

V.

The *Fourth* reached out his eager hand,
    And felt about the knee ;
" What most this wondrous beast is like
    Is mighty plain," quoth he ;
" 'T is clear enough the Elephant
    Is very like a tree ! "

VI.

The *Fifth*, who chanced to touch the ear,
    Said, " E'en the blindest man
Can tell what this resembles most :
    Deny the fact who can,
This marvel of an Elephant
    Is very like a fan ! "

VII.

The *Sixth* no sooner had begun
    About the beast to grope,
Than, seizing on the swinging tail
    That fell within his scope,
" I see," quoth he, "the Elephant
    Is very like a rope ! "

VIII.

And so these men of Indostan
  Disputed loud and long,
Each in his own opinion
  Exceeding stiff and strong,
Though each was partly in the right,
  And all were in the wrong!

MORAL.

So, oft in theologic wars
  The disputants, I ween,
Rail on in utter ignorance
  Of what each other mean,
And prate about an Elephant
  Not one of them has seen!

THE CALIPH AND THE CRIPPLE.

AN ARABIAN TALE.

THE CALIPH AND THE CRIPPLE.

AN ARABIAN TALE.

I.

HE Caliph BEN AKAS, — whose surname was " Wise,"
  From the wisdom and wit he displayed, —
One morning rode forth in a merchant's disguise
  To see how his laws were obeyed.

II.

While riding along, in a leisurely way,
  A beggar came up to his side,
And said, " In the name of the Prophet, I pray
  You 'll give a poor cripple a ride."

III.

Ben Akas, amazed at the mendicant's prayer,
  Asked where he was wishing to go ;
" I 'm going," he said, "to the neighboring fair ;
  But my crutches are wretchedly slow."

IV.

" Get up ! " said the Caliph, — "a saddle like this
  Is hardly sufficient for two ;
And yet, by the Prophet ! 't were greatly amiss
  To snub a poor cripple like you ! "

V.

The beggar got up, and together they rode
  Till they came to the neighboring town,
When, hard by the house where the *Cadi* abode,
  He bade his companion get down.

VI.

" Nay, get down *yourself!* " was the fellow's reply,
   Without the least shame or remorse ;
" Indeed !" said the Caliph, " and pray tell me why ?"
   Quoth the beggar, " To give me the horse !

VII.

" You know very well that the nag is my own ;
   And if you resort to the laws,
You do not imagine your story alone
   Sufficient to carry the cause ?

VIII.

" The Cadi is reckoned the wisest of men,
   And, looking at you and at me,
After hearing us both, 't is a hundred to ten
   The cripple will get the decree."

IX.

" Very well !" said Ben Akas, — astonished to hear
   The impudent fellow's discourse, —
" If the Cadi is wise, there is little to fear
   But I soon shall recover my horse."

X.

"Agreed!" said the beggar, — "whate'er the decree,
  The verdict shall find me content";
" As to that," said the other, "we 'll presently see";
  And so to the Cadi they went.

XI.

It chanced that a cause was engrossing the Cadi,
  Where a woman occasioned the strife;
And both parties claimed the identical lady
  As being his own lawful wife.

XII.

The one was a peasant; a scholar the other;
  And each made a speech in his turn;
But — what was a very particular bother —
  The woman refused to be sworn.

XIII.

" Enough for the present!" the Cadi declared,
  "Come back in the morning," said he;
" And now" (to Ben Akas) "the Court is prepared
  To hear what your grievance may be!"

XIV.

Ben Akas no sooner the truth had narrated,
　When the beggar as coolly replies,
" I swear, by the Prophet ! the fellow has stated
　A parcel of impudent lies !

XV.

" I was coming to market, and when I descried
　A man by the wayside alone,
Looking weary and faint, — why, I gave him a ride :
　Now he swears that the horse is his own ! "

XVI.

" Very well," said the Judge, "let us go to the stable
　And each shall select in his turn."
Ben Akas went first, and was easily able
　His favorite steed to discern.

XVII.

The cripple went next ; though the stable was full,
　The true one was instantly shown ;
" Your Honor," said he, "did you think me so dull
　That I could n't distinguish my own ? "

XVIII.

Next morning the Cadi came into the court,
  And sat himself down at his ease ;
And thither the suitors and people resort
  To list to the Judge's decrees.

XIX.

First calling the Scholar, who sued for his spouse,
  His Honor thus settled the doubt : —
" The woman is yours ; take her home to your house,
  And don't let her often go out."

XX.

Then calling before him Ben Akas, — whose cause
  Stood next in the calendar's course, —
He said : " By the Prophet's inflexible laws,
  Let the merchant recover his horse !

XXI.

" And as for the beggar, I further decide
  His villany fairly has earned
A good hundred lashes well laid on his hide ;
  Meshallah ! The court is adjourned !"

XXII.

Ben Akas that night sought the Cadi's abode,
　And said, " 'T is the CALIPH you see !
Though hither, indeed, as a merchant I rode,
　I am ABOU BEN AKAS to thee ! "

XXIII.

The Cadi, abashed, made the lowest of bows,
　And, kissing his Majesty's hand,
Cried, " Great is the honor you do to my house ;
　I wait for your royal command ! "

XXIV.

" I fain would possess," was the Caliph's reply,
　" Your wisdom ; so tell me, I pray,
How your Honor discovered where justice might lie
　In the causes decided to-day."

XXV.

" Why, as to the woman," the Cadi replied,
　" It was easily settled, I think ;
Just taking the lady a moment aside,
　I said, ' Fill my standish with ink.'

XXVI.

" And quick, at the order, the bottle was taken,
  With a dainty and dexterous hold ;
The standish was washed ; the fluid was shaken ;
  New cotton put in for the old — "

XXVII.

" I see !" said the Caliph ; " the story is pleasant ;
  Of course it was easy to tell
The Scholar swore truly, — the spouse of a peasant
  Could never have done it so well.

XXVIII.

And now for the horse ?" " That was harder, I own,
  For, mark you, the beggarly elf
(However the rascal may chance to have known)
  Knew the palfrey as well as yourself !

XXIX.

" But the truth was apparent, the moment I learned
  What the animal thought of the two ;
The impudent cripple he savagely spurned,
  But was plainly delighted with you !"

XXX.

Ben Akas sat musing and silent awhile,
  As one whom devotion employs;
Then, raising his head with a heavenly smile,
  He said, in a reverent voice : —

XXXI.

" Sure, Allah is good and abundant in grace!
  Thy wisdom is greater than mine ;
I would that the Caliph might rule in his place
  As well as thou servest in thine!"

THE PIOUS BRAHMIN AND HIS NEIGHBORS.

A HINDOO FABLE.

THE PIOUS BRAHMIN AND HIS NEIGH-BORS.

A HINDOO FABLE.

I.

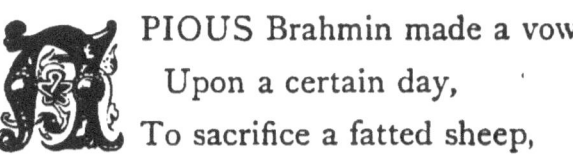 PIOUS Brahmin made a vow
    Upon a certain day,
To sacrifice a fatted sheep,
  And so, his vow to pay,
One morning to the market-place
  The Brahmin took his way.

II.

It chanced three cunning neighbors,
    Three rogues of brazen brow,
Had formed the wicked purpose
    (My tale will tell you how)
To cheat the pious Brahmin,
    And profit by his vow.

III.

The leader of these cunning knaves
    Went forth upon the road,
And, bearing on his shoulders
    What seemed a heavy load,
He met the pious Brahmin
    Not far from his abode.

IV.

"What have you there?" the Brahmin said.
    "Indeed," the man replies,
"I have the finest, fattest sheep,
    And of the largest size;
A sheep well worthy to be slain
    In solemn sacrifice!"

V.

And then the rogue laid down his load,
    And from a bag drew forth
A scurvy dog ! — " See there ! " he cried,
    " The finest sheep on earth !
And you shall have him, if you will,
    For less than he is worth."

VI.

" Wretch ! " cried the pious Brahmin,
    " To call a beast so mean
A goodly sheep !   'T is but a dog,
    Accurséd and unclean ;
The foulest, leanest, lamest cur
    That ever yet was seen ! "

VII.

Just then the second rogue came up :
    " What luck ! " he said, " to find
So soon a sheep in flesh and fleece
    Exactly to my mind ! "
" A sheep ? " exclaimed the Brahmin,
    " Then I am surely blind ! "

VIII.

"You must be very blind indeed,
  Or fond of telling lies,
To say the beast is *not* a sheep!"
  The cunning rogue replies;
"Go get a leech to mend your tongue,
  Or else to mend your eyes!"

IX.

Now while these men disputed thus,
  The other rogue drew near,
And all agreed this honest man
  Should make the matter clear.
"O stranger!" cried the Brahmin,
  "What creature have we here?"

X.

"A goodly sheep!" the stranger said.
  "Alas!" the Brahmin cried,
"A moment since I would have sworn
  This honest fellow lied;
But now I know it is a sheep,
  Since thus you all decide."

XI.

And so it was the cunning knaves
   Prevailed in their device ;
The pious Brahmin bought the dog,
   Nor higgled at the price ;
"'T will make," he said, "unto the gods
   A pleasing sacrifice !"

XII.

But ill betide the fatal hour
   His filthy blood was shed ;
It brought no benison, alas !
   Upon the Brahmin's head ;
The gods were angry at the deed,
   And sent a curse instead.

XIII.

The meaning of this pleasant tale
   Is very plainly shown ;
The man is sure to fall at last
   Who does n't stand alone ;
Don't trust to other people's eyes,
   But learn to mind your own.

THE THREE GIFTS.

A TALE OF NORTH GERMANY.

THE THREE GIFTS.

A TALE OF NORTH GERMANY.

I.

THREE gentlemen mounted their horses
one day,
And far in the country they rode,
Till they came to a cottage that stood by the way,
Where an honest old weaver abode.

II.

This honest old weaver was wretchedly poor,
  Yet he never was surly nor sad ;
He welcomed the travellers into his door,
  And gave them the best that he had.

III.

They ate and they drank till the weaver began
  To fear that they never would cease ;
But when they had finished, they gave to the man
  A hundred gold guineas apiece.

IV.

Then the gentlemen mounted their horses again,
  And, bidding the weaver "Good night,"
Went dashing away over valley and plain,
  And were presently lost to his sight.

V.

Sure never was weaver so happy before,
  And never seemed guineas so bright ;
He counted the pieces a hundred times o'er,
  With more than a miser's delight.

VI.

Then snug in some rags he hid them away,
  As if he had got them by stealth,
Lest his meddlesome wife, who was absent that day,
  Should know of his wonderful wealth.

VII.

Soon after a travelling rag-dealer came,
  The rags in the bundle were sold,
And with them (the woman was little to blame!)
  The three hundred guineas of gold.

VIII.

When a calendar year had vanished and fled,
  The gentlemen came as before;
" Now how does it happen," they moodily said,
  " We find you so wretchedly poor?"

IX.

" Alas!" said the weaver, " this many a day
  The money is missing, in sooth;
In a bundle of rags it was hidden away,
  ('Fore God! — I am telling the truth!)

X.

" But once, in my absence, a rag-dealer came,
   The rags in the bundle were sold,
And with them (the woman was surely to blame !)
   The three hundred guineas of gold."

XI.

" It was foolishly done," the gentlemen swore ;
   " Now, prithee, be careful of these " ;
And they gave him again — the same as before —
   A hundred gold guineas apiece.

XII.

Then the gentlemen mounted their horses again,
   And, bidding the weaver " Good night,"
Went dashing away over valley and plain,
   And were presently lost to his sight.

XIII.

" I' faith ! " said the weaver, " no wonder they chid ;
   But now I am wiser, I trust " ;
So the three hundred guineas he carefully hid
   Far down in a barrel of dust.

XIV.

But soon, in his absence, a dustman came,
　　The dust in the barrel was sold ;
And with it (the woman was little to blame !)
　　The three hundred guineas of gold.

XV.

When a calendar year had vanished and fled,
　　The gentlemen came as before ;
" Now how does it happen," they angrily said,
　　" We find you so wretchedly poor ? "

XVI.

" Was ever," he cried, " so luckless a wight ?
　　As surely as Heaven is just,
The money I hid from my spouse's sight
　　Far down in a barrel of dust ;

XVII.

" But when I was absent the dustman came,
　　The dust in the barrel was sold,
And with it (the woman was surely to blame !)
　　The three hundred guineas of gold."

XVIII.

"Take that for your folly!" the gentlemen said;
  "Was ever so silly a wight?"
And they tossed on the table a lump of lead,
  And were presently out of his sight.

XIX.

"'T is plain," said the weaver, "they meant to flout
  And little I marvel; alas! —
My wife is a fool; and there is n't a doubt
  That I am an arrant ass!"

XX.

While thus he was musing in sorrow and shame,
  And wishing that he was dead,
Into his cottage a fisherman came
  To borrow a lump of lead.

XXI.

"Ah! here," he cried, "is the thing I wish
  To mend my broken net;
Will you give it me for the finest fish
  That I this day may get?"

XXII.

" With all my heart !" the weaver replies ;
  And so the fisherman brought
That night a fish of wondrous size, —
  The finest that he had caught.

XXIII.

He opened the fish, when lo and behold !
  He found a precious stone ;
A diamond large as the lead he sold,
  And bright as the morning sun !

XXIV.

For a thousand guineas the stone he sold,
  (It was worth a hundred more,)
And never, 't is said, in bliss or gold,
  Was weaver so rich before !

XXV.

But often — to keep her sway, no doubt,
  As a genuine woman must —
The wife would say, " *I* brought it about
  By selling the rags and dust !"

THE YOUTH AND THE NORTH-WIND.

A TALE OF NORWAY.

THE YOUTH AND THE NORTH-WIND.

A TALE OF NORWAY.

I.

NCE on a time — 't was long ago —
There lived a worthy dame
Who sent her son to fetch some flour,
For she was old and lame.

II.

But while he loitered on the road,
  The North-wind chanced to stray
Across the careless younker's path,
  And stole the flour away.

III.

" Alas ! what shall we do for bread ? "
  Exclaimed the weeping lad ;
" The flour is gone ! — the flour is gone ! —
  And it was all we had ! "

IV.

And so he sought the North-wind's cave
  Beside the distant main ;
" Good Master Boreas ! " said the lad,
  " I want my flour again !

V.

" 'T was all we had to live upon, —
  My mother old and I ;
O give us back the flour again,
  Or we shall surely die ! "

VI.

"I have it not," the North-wind growled,
    "But for your lack of bread,
I give to you this table-cloth ;
    'T will serve you well instead :

VII.

"For you have but to spread it out,
    And every costly dish
Will straight appear at your command,
    Whatever you may wish."

VIII.

The lad received the magic cloth
    With wonder and delight,
And thanked the donor heartily,
    As well indeed he might.

IX.

Returning homeward, at an inn
    Just half his journey through,
He fain must show his table-cloth,
    And what the cloth could do.

X.

So, while he slept, the knavish host
      Went slyly to his bed,
And stole the cloth, — but shrewdly placed
      Another in its stead.

XI.

Unknowing what the rogue had done,
      The lad went on his way,
And came unto his journey's end
      Just at the close of day.

XII.

He showed the dame his table-cloth,
      And told her of its power ;
" Good sooth ! " he cried, " 't was well for us
      The North-wind stole the flour ! "

XIII.

" Perhaps," exclaimed the cautious crone,
      " The story may be true ;
'T is mighty little good, I ween,
      Your table-cloth can do ! "

XIV.

And now the younker spread it forth,
    And tried the spell, — alas !
'T was but a common table-cloth,
    And nothing came to pass.

XV.

Then to the North-wind, far away,
    He sped with might and main ;
" Your table-cloth is good for naught :
    I want my flour again ! "

XVI.

" I have it not," the North-wind growled,
    " But, for your lack of bread,
I give to you this little goat,
    'T will serve you well instead ;

XVII.

" For you have but to tell him this :
    'Make money ! Master Bill !'
And he will give you golden coins,
    As many as you will ! "

XVIII.

The lad received the magic goat,
    With wonder and delight,
And thanked the donor heartily,
    As well indeed he might.

XIX.

Returning homeward, at the inn
    Just half his journey through,
He fain must show his little goat,
    And what the goat could do.

XX.

So while he slept, the knavish host
    Went slyly to the shed,
And stole the goat, — but shrewdly placed
    Another in his stead.

XXI.

Unknowing what the rogue had done,
    The youth went on his way,
And reached his weary journey's end
    Just at the close of day.

XXII.

He showed the dame his magic goat,
    And told her of his power ;
" Good sooth !" he cried, " 't was well for us
    The North-wind stole the flour !"

XXIII.

" I much misdoubt," the dame replied,
    " Your wondrous tale is true :
'T is little good, for hungry folk,
    Your silly goat can do !"

XXIV.

" Good Master Bill !" the lad exclaimed,
    " Make money !" — but, alas !
'T was nothing but a common goat,
    And nothing came to pass !

XXV.

Then to the North-wind, angrily,
    He sped with might and main :
" Your foolish goat is good for naught :
    I want my flour again !"

XXVI.

" I have it not," the North-wind growled,
　" Nor can I give you aught,
Except this cudgel, — which, indeed,
　A magic charm has got ;

XXVII.

" For you have but to tell it this :
　' My cudgel ! hit away !'
And, till you bid it stop again,
　The cudgel will obey."

XXVIII.

Returning home, he stopped at night
　Where he had lodged before ;
And feigning to be fast asleep,
　He soon began to snore.

XXIX.

And when the host would steal the staff,
　The sleeper muttered, " Stay, —
I see what you would fain be at ;
　Good cudgel ! hit away !"

XXX.

The cudgel thumped about his ears,
  Till he began to cry,
"O stop the staff, for mercy's sake!
  Or I shall surely die!"

XXXI.

But still the cudgel thumped away
  Until the rascal said,
"I'll give you back the cloth and goat:
  O spare my broken head!"

XXXII.

And so it was the lad reclaimed
  His table-cloth and goat;
And, growing rich, at length became
  A man of famous note.

XXXIII.

He kept his mother tenderly,
  And cheered her waning life;
And married — as you may suppose —
  A princess for a wife;

XXXIV.

And while he lived had ever near,
   To favor worthy ends,
A cudgel for his enemies,
   And money for his friends!

THE UGLY AUNT.

A TALE FROM THE NORWEGIAN.

THE UGLY AUNT.

A TALE FROM THE NORWEGIAN

I.

T was a little maiden
 Lived long and long ago,
 (Though when it was, and where it was,
 I 'm sure I do not know,)
And her face was all the fortune
 This maiden had to show.

II.

And yet — what many people
　　Will think extremely rare
In one who, like this maiden,
　　Ne'er knew a mother's care —
The neighbors all asserted
　　That she was good as fair.

III.

" Alack ! " exclaimed the damsel,
　　While bitter tears she shed,
" I 'm little skilled to labor,
　　And yet I must be fed ;
I fain by daily service
　　Would earn my daily bread."

IV.

And so she sought a palace
　　Where dwelt a mighty queen,
And when the royal lady
　　The little maid had seen,
She loved her for her beauty,
　　Despite her lowly mien.

V.

Not long she served her Majesty
   Ere jealousy arose,
(Because she was the favorite,
   As you may well suppose,)
And all the other servants
   Became her bitter foes.

VI.

And so these false companions,
   In envy of her face,
Contrived a wicked stratagem
   To bring her to disgrace,
And fill her soul with sorrow,
   And rob her of her place.

VII.

They told her royal Majesty,
   (Most arrant liars they !)
That often, in their gossiping,
   They 'd heard the maiden say
That she could spin a pound of flax
   All in a single day !

VIII.

"Indeed!" exclaimed her Majesty,
  "I'm fond of spinning, too;
So come, my little maiden,
  And make your boasting true;
Or else your foolish vanity
  You presently may rue!"

IX.

Alas! the hapless damsel
  Was now afflicted sore:
No mother e'er had taught her
  In such ingenious lore;
A spinning-wheel in all her life
  She ne'er had seen before.

X.

But fearing much to tell the queen
  How she had been belied,
She tried to spin upon the wheel,
  And still in vain she tried;
And so — 't was all that she could do —
  She sat her down and cried.

XI.

Now while she thus laments her fate
    In sorrow deep and wild,
A beldam stands before her view,
    And says, in accents mild,
" What ails thee now, my pretty one,
    Say, what 's the matter, child ! "

XII.

Soon as she heard the piteous case,
    " Cheer up ! " the beldam said,
" I 'll spin for thee the pound of flax,
    And thou shalt go to bed,
If only thou wilt call me ' Aunt,'
    The day that thou art wed ! "

XIII.

The maiden promised true and fair,
    And when the day was done,
The queen went in to see the task,
    And found it fairly spun ;
Quoth she, " I love thee passing well,
    And thou shalt wed my son !

XIV.

" For one who spins so well as thee,
  (In sooth ! 't is wondrous fine !)
With beauty, too, so very rare,
  And goodness such as thine,
Should be the daughter of a queen,
  And I will have thee mine !"

XV.

Now when the wedding-day had come,
  And, decked in royal pride,
Around the smoking table sat
  The bridegroom and the bride,
With all the royal kinsfolk,
  And many guests beside,

XVI.

In came a beldam, with a frisk ;
  Was ever dame so bold ?
Or one so lean and wrinkled,
  So ugly and so old,'
Or with a nose so very long
  And shocking to behold ?

XVII.

Now while they sat in wonderment
　This curious dame to see,
She said unto the Princess,
　As bold as bold could be,
" Good morrow, gentle lady ! "
　" Good morrow, *Aunt !* " quoth she.

XVIII.

The Prince with gay demeanor,
　But with an inward groan,
Then bade her sit at table,
　And said, in friendly tone,
" If you 're my bride's relation,
　Why then you are my own ! "

XIX.

When dinner now was ended,
　As you may well suppose,
The Prince still thought about his *Aunt*,
　And still his wonder rose
Where could the ugly beldam
　Have got so long a nose !

XX.

At last he plainly asked her,
  Before that merry throng,
And she as plainly answered,
  (Nor deemed his freedom wrong,)
" 'T was spinning in my girlhood
  That made my nose so long ! "

XXI.

" Indeed ! " exclaimed his Highness,
  And then and there he swore,
" Though spinning made me husband
  To her whom I adore,
Lest she should spoil her beauty,
  Why, she shall spin no more ! " *

---

* If the present version is more simple in plot than the prose story
in the "*Norske Folkeœventer*," it certainly gains something in refine-
ment by the variation.

HO-HO OF THE GOLDEN BELT.

ONE OF THE "NINE STORIES OF CHINA."

HO-HO OF THE GOLDEN BELT.

ONE OF THE "NINE STORIES OF CHINA."

BEAUTIFUL maiden was little Min-Ne,
Eldest daughter of wise Wang-Ke;
Her skin had the color of saffron tea,
And her nose was flat as flat could be;
And never were seen such beautiful eyes,
Two almond-kernels in shape and size,

Set in a couple of slanting gashes,
And not in the least disfigured by lashes ;
      And then such feet !
      You 'd scarcely meet
In the longest walk through the grandest street
      (And you might go seeking
      From Nanking to Peeking)
A pair so remarkably small and neat

      Two little stumps,
      Mere pedal lumps,
That toddle along with the funniest thumps,
In China, you know, are reckoned trumps.
It seems a trifle, to make such a boast of it ;
      But how they *will* dress it,
      And bandage and press it,
By making the least, to make the most of it !

      As you may suppose,
      She had plenty of beaux
Bowing around her beautiful toes,
Praising her feet, and eyes, and nose
In rapturous verse and elegant prose !

She had lots of lovers, old and young ;
There was lofty LONG, and babbling LUNG,
Opulent TIN, and eloquent TUNG,
Musical SING, and, the rest among,
Great HANG-YU and YU-BE-HUNG.

But though they smiled and smirked and bowed,
None could please her of all the crowd ;
LUNG and TUNG she thought too loud ;
Opulent TIN was much too proud ;
Lofty LONG was quite too tall ;
Musical SING sung very small ;
And, most remarkable freak of all,
Of great HANG-YU the lady made game,
And YU-BE-HUNG she mocked the same,
By echoing back his ugly name !

But the hardest heart is doomed to melt ;
Love is a passion that *will* be felt ;
And just when scandal was making free
To hint " what a pretty old maid she 'd be," —
Little *Min-Ne*,
Who but she ?

Married Ho-Ho of the Golden Belt!
A man, I must own, of bad reputation,
And low in purse, though high in station, —
A sort of Imperial poor-relation,
Who ranked as the Emperor's second cousin
Multiplied by a hundred dozen ;
And, to mark the love the Emperor felt,

Had a pension clear
Of three pounds a year,

And the honor of wearing a Golden Belt !

And gallant Ho-Ho
Could really show

A handsome face, as faces go
In this Flowery Land, where, you must know,
The finest flowers of beauty grow.
He 'd the very widest kind of jaws,
And his nails were like an eagle's claws,
And — though it may seem a wondrous tail —
(Truth is mighty and will prevail !)
He 'd a *queue* as long as the deepest cause
Under the Emperor's chancery-laws !

Yet how he managed to win MIN-NE
The men declared they could n't see ;
But all the ladies, over their tea,
In this one point were known to agree : —
Four gifts were sent to aid his plea :
A smoking-pipe with a golden clog,
A box of tea, and a poodle dog,
And a painted heart that was all a-flame,
And bore, in blood, the lover's name.

Ah ! how could presents pretty as these
A delicate lady fail to please ?
She smoked the pipe with the golden clog,
And drank the tea, and ate the dog,
And kept the heart, — and that 's the way
The match was made, the gossips say.

I can't describe the wedding day,
Which fell in the lovely month of May ;
Nor stop to tell of the Honey-Moon,
And how it vanished all too soon ;
Alas ! that I the truth must speak,
And say that in the fourteenth week,

Soon as the wedding-guests were gone,
   And their wedding-suits began to doff,
Min-Ne was weeping and "taking on,"
   For *he* had been trying to "take her off!"

Six wives before he had sent to Heaven,
And being partial to number "Seven,"
He wished to add his latest pet,
Just, perhaps, to make up the set!
Mayhap the rascal found a cause
Of discontent in a certain clause
In the Emperor's very liberal laws,
Which gives, when a Golden Belt is wed,
Six hundred pounds to furnish the bed;
And if in turn he marry a score,
With every wife six hundred more.

First he tried to murder Min-Ne
With a special cup of poisoned tea;
But the lady, smelling a mortal foe,
     Cried, "Ho-Ho!
I 'm very fond of mild Souchong,
But you — my love — you make it too strong!"

At last Ho-Ho, the treacherous man,
Contrived the most infernal plan
Invented since the world began :
He went and got him a savage dog,
Who 'd eat a woman as soon as a frog,
Kept him a day without any prog,
Then shut him up in an iron bin,
Slipped the bolt, and locked him in ;

> Then giving the key
> To poor MIN-NE,

Said, " Love, there 's something you *must n't* see
In the chest beneath the orange-tree."

*   *   *   *   *

Poor, mangled MIN-NE ! with her latest breath,
She told her father the cause of her death ;
And so it reached the Emperor's ear,
And his Highness said, " It is very clear,
Ho-Ho has committed a murder here ! "

And he doomed Ho-Ho to end his life
By the terrible dog that killed his wife ;
But in mercy (let his praise be sung !)
His thirteen brothers were merely hung,

And his slaves bambooed, in the mildest way,
For a calendar month, three times a day,
And that 's the way that JUSTICE dealt
With wicked Ho-Ho of the Golden Belt!

RAMPSINITUS AND THE ROBBER.

AN EGYPTIAN TALE.

RAMPSINITUS AND THE ROBBER.

AN EGYPTIAN TALE.

I.

KING Rampsinitus was a prince
    Who lived in days of old,
    And finding that his treasury
Was quite too small to hold
His jewels and his money-bags
    Of silver and of gold,

II.

He built a secret chamber,
　　With this intent alone,
(That is, he got an architect
　　And caused it to be done,)
A most substantial structure
　　Of mortar and of stone.

III.

A very solid building
　　It appeared to every eye,
Except the master-mason's,
　　Who plainly could espy
One stone that fitted loosely
　　When the masonry was dry.

IV.

A dozen years had vanished,
　　When, in the common way,
The architect was summoned
　　His final debt to pay,
And thus unto his children
　　The dying man did say : —

V.

"Come hither now, my darling sons,
　Come, list my children twain,
I have a little secret
　I am going to explain ;
'T is a comfort, now I 'm dying,
　That I have n't lived in vain."

VI.

And then he plainly told them
　Of the trick that he had done :
How in the royal chamber
　He had put a sliding stone, —
"You 'll find it near the bottom,
　On the side that 's next the sun.

VII.

"Now I feel that I am going :
　Swift ebbs the vital tide ;
No longer in this wicked world
　My spirit may abide ! "
And so this worthy gentleman
　Turned up his toes and died !

VIII.

It was n't long before the sons
   Improved the father's hint,
And searched the secret chamber
   To discover what was in 't ;
And found, by self-promotion,
   They were " Masters of the Mint ! "

IX.

At length King RAMPSINITUS
   Perceived, as well he might,
His caskets and his money-bags
   Were getting rather light ;
" And yet," quoth he, " my bolts and bars
   Are all exactly right !

X.

" I wonder how the cunning dog
   Has managed to get in ;
However, it is clear enough
   I 'm losing lots of tin ;
I 'll try the virtue of a trap
   Before the largest bin ! "

XI.

In came the thief that very night,
  And soon the other chap,
Who waited at the opening,
  On hearing something snap,
Went in and found his brother
  A-sitting in the trap !

XII.

" You see me in a pretty fix !"
  The gallant fellow said ;
" 'T is better, now, that one should die
  Than two of us be dead :
Lest both should be detected,
  Cut off my foolish head ! "

XIII.

" Indeed," replied the other,
  " Such a cut were hardly kind,
And to obey your order
  I am truly disinclined ;
But, as you 're the elder brother,
  I suppose I ought to mind."

XIV.

So with his iron hanger
    He severed, at a slap,
The noddle of the victim,
    Which he carried through the gap,
And left the bleeding body
    A-sitting in the trap.

XV.

His Majesty's amazement
    Of course was very great,
On entering the chamber
    That held his cash and plate,
To find the robber's body
    Without a bit of pate !

XVI.

To solve the mighty mystery
    Was now his whole intent ;
And everywhere, to find the head,
    His officers were sent ;
But every man came back again
    No wiser than he went.

XVII.

At last he set a dozen men
　The mystery to trace ;
And bade them watch the body
　In a very public place,
And note what signs of sorrow
　They might see in any face.

XVIII.

The robber, guessing what it meant,
　Was naturally shy ;
And though he mingled in the crowd,
　Took care to "mind his eye,"
For fear his brother's body-guard
　His sorrow should espy.

XIX.

" I 'll cheat 'em yet ! " the fellow said,
　And so that very night
He planned a cunning stratagem
　To get the soldiers " tight,"
And steal away his brother's trunk
　Before the morning light.

XX.

He got a dozen asses,
  And put upon their backs
As many loads as donkeys
  Of wine in leather-sacks ;
Then set the bags a-leaking
  From a dozen little cracks.

XXI.

Then going where the soldiers
  Were keeping watch and ward,
The fellows saw the leaking wine
  With covetous regard,
And straitway fell a-drinking,
  And drank extremely hard.

XXII.

The owner stormed and scolded
  With well-affected spunk,
But still they kept a-drinking
  Till all of them were drunk ;
And so it was the robber
  Stole off his brother's trunk !

XXIII.

Now when King RAMPSINITUS
　　Had heard the latest news,
'T is said his royal Majesty
　　Expressed his royal views
In language such as gentlemen
　　Are seldom known to use !

XXIV.

Now when a year had vanished,
　　He formed another plan
To catch the chap who 'd stolen
　　The mutilated man ;
And summoning the Princess,
　　His Majesty began : —

XXV.

" My daughter, hold a masquerade
　　And offer — as in fun —
Five kisses (in your chamber)
　　To every mother's son
Who will tell the shrewdest mischief
　　That he ever yet has done.

XXVI.

"If you chance to find the robber
  By the trick that I have planned,
Remember, on the instant,
  You must seize him by the hand,
Then await such further orders
  As your father may command."

XXVII.

The Princess made the party,
  Without the least dissent ;
'T was a general invitation,
  And everybody went, —
The robber with the others,
  Though he guessed the king's intent.

XXVIII.

Now when the cunning robber
  Was questioned, like the rest,
He said, " Your Royal Highness,
  I solemnly protest
Of all my subtle rogueries,
  I scarce know which is best :

XXIX.

" But I venture the opinion,
  'T was a rather pretty job,
When, having with my hanger
  Cut off my brother's nob,
I managed from the soldiers
  His headless trunk to rob ! "

XXX.

And now the frightened Princess
  Gave a very heavy groan,
For, to her consternation,
  The cunning thief had flown,
And left the hand she grappled
  Still lying in her own !

XXXI.

(For he a hand had borrowed,
  'T is needful to be said,
From the body of a gentleman
  That recently was dead,
And *that* he gave the Princess
  The moment that he fled !)

XXXII.

Then good King RAMPSINITUS
    Incontinently swore
That this paragon of robbers
    He would persecute no more ;
For such a clever rascal
    Had never lived before !

XXXIII.

And in that goodly company
    His Majesty declared,
That, if the thief would show himself,
    His person should be spared,
And with his only daughter
    In marriage should be paired !

XXXIV.

And when King RAMPSINITUS
    Had run his mortal lease,
He left them in his testament
    Just half a crown apiece :
May ever modest merit
    Thus flourish and increase !

THE WANDERING JEW.

A BALLAD.

THE WANDERING JEW.

A BALLAD.

I.

COME list, my dear,
And you shall hear
About the wonderful Wandering Jew,
Who night and day,
The legends say,
Is taking a journey he never gets through.

II.

What is his name,
Or whence he came,
Or whither the weary wanderer goes ;
Or why he should stray
In this singular way,
Many have marvelled, but nobody knows.

III.

Though oft, indeed,
(As you may read
In ancient histories quaint and true,)
A man is seen
Of haggard mien
Whom people call the Wandering Jew.

IV.

Once in Brabant,
With garments scant,
And shoeless feet, a stranger appeared ;
His step was slow,
And white as snow
Were his waving locks and flowing beard.

V.

His cheek was spare,

His head was bare,

And little he recked of heat or cold;

Misfortune's trace

Was in his face,

And he seemed at least a century old.

VI.

" Now, goodman, bide,"

The people cried,

" The night with us, — it were surely best ;

The wind is cold,

And thou art old,

And sorely needest shelter and rest ! "

VII.

"Thanks! thanks!" said he,

" It may not be

That I should tarry the night with you ;

I cannot stay ;

I must away,

For I, alas! am the Wandering Jew ! "

VIII.

" We oft have read,"
The people said,
" Thou bearest ever a nameless woe ;
Now, prithee tell
How it befell
That thou art always wandering so ? "

IX.

" The time would fail
To tell my tale,
And yet a little, ere I depart,
Would I relate
About my fate,
For some — perhaps — may lay it to heart.

X.

" When but a youth,
(And such, in sooth,
Are ever of giddy and wanton mood,)
With tearless eye
I saw pass by
The Saviour bearing the hateful rood.

XI.

"And when he stooped,
And, groaning, drooped
And staggered and fell beneath the weight,
I cursed his name,
And cried, 'For shame!
Move on, blasphemer, and meet thy fate!'

XII.

"He raised his head,
And, smiling, said:
'Move on thyself! In sorrow and pain,
When I am gone,
Shalt thou move on,
Nor rest thy foot till I come again!'

XIII.

"Alas! the time
That saw my crime —
('T was more than a thousand years ago!)
And since that hour
Some inward power
Has kept me wandering to and fro.

XIV.

" I fain would die
That I might lie
With those who sleep in the silent tomb ;
But not for me
Is rest — till He
Shall come to end my dreadful doom.

XV.

" The pestilence
That hurries hence
A thousand souls in a single night,
Brings me no death
Upon its breath,
But passes by in its wayward flight.

XVI.

" The storm that wrecks
An hundred decks,
And drowns the shuddering, shrieking crew,
Still leaves afloat
The fragile boat
That bears the life of the Wandering Jew.

XVII.

"But I must away ;
I cannot stay ;
Nor further suffer a moment's loss ;
Heed well the word
That ye have heard, —
Nor spurn the Saviour who bore the Cross !" *

* The tradition of the Wandering Jew is very old and popular in every country of Europe, and is the theme of many modern works of fiction, of which the most famous are Lewis's "Monk," Southey's "Curse of Kehama," Croly's "Salathiel," a romance by Goethe, and a novel by Sué. The old Spanish writers make the narrative as diabolical and revolting as possible, while the French and Flemish authors soften the legend (as in the present ballad) into a pathetic story of sin, suffering, and genuine repentance.

THE ROMANCE OF NICK VAN STANN.

THE ROMANCE OF NICK VAN STANN.

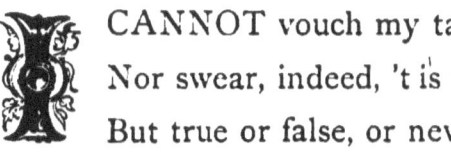 CANNOT vouch my tale is true,
Nor swear, indeed, 't is wholly new ;
But true or false, or new or old,
I think you 'll find it fairly told.

A Frenchman who had ne'er before
Set foot upon a foreign shore,

Weary of home, resolved to go
And see what Holland had to show.
He did n't know a word of Dutch,
But that could hardly grieve him much ;
He thought — as Frenchmen always do —
That all the world could "*parley-voo.*"

At length our eager tourist stands
Within the famous Netherlands,
And, strolling gayly here and there
In search of something rich or rare,
A lordly mansion greets his eyes ;
" How beautiful ! " the Frenchman cries,
And, bowing to the man who sat
In livery at the garden-gate,
" Pray, Mr. Porter, if you please,
Whose very charming grounds are these ?
And — pardon me — be pleased to tell
Who in this splendid house may dwell ? "
To which, in Dutch, the puzzled man
Replied what seemed like " *Nick Van Stann.*" *

* *Niet verstaan* = don't understand.

"Thanks!" said the Gaul, "the owner's taste
Is equally superb and chaste ;
So fine a house, upon my word,
Not even Paris can afford.
With statues, too, in every niche,
Of course, *Monsieur Van Stann* is rich,
And lives, I warrant, like a king, —
Ah ! wealth must be a charming thing !"

In Amsterdam the Frenchman meets
A thousand wonders in the streets,
But most he marvels to behold
A lady dressed in silk and gold.
Gazing with rapture at the dame,
He begs to know the lady's name,
And hears — to raise his wonder more —
The very words he heard before !
"*Mercie !*" he cries, "well, on my life,
Milord has got a charming wife ;
'T is plain to see, this *Nick Van Stann*
Must be a very happy man !"

Next day, our tourist chanced to pop
His head within a lottery-shop,

And there he saw, with staring eyes,
The drawing of the Mammoth Prize.
" Ten Millions ! — 'T is a pretty sum ;
I wish I had as much at home !
I 'd like to know, as I 'm a sinner,
What lucky fellow is the winner ? "
Conceive our traveller's amaze
To hear again the hackneyed phrase !
" What ! No ? — not *Nick Van Stann* again ?
Faith ! he 's the luckiest of men !
You may be sure we don't advance
So rapidly as that in France !
A house, the finest in the land ;
A lovely garden, nicely planned ;
A perfect angel of a wife,
And gold enough to last a life, —
There never yet was mortal man
So very blessed as *Nick Van Stann !* "

Next day the Frenchman chanced to meet
A pompous funeral in the street,
And, asking one who stood near by
What nobleman had pleased to die,
Was stunned to hear the old reply !

The Frenchman sighed and shook his head,
" *Mon Dieu !* poor *Nick Van Stann* is dead !
With such a house, and such a wife,
It must be hard to part with life ;
And then, to lose that Mammoth Prize !
He wins, and — pop ! — the winner dies !
Ah ! well, — his blessings came so fast,
I greatly feared they couldn' t last ;
And thus, we see, the sword of Fate
Cuts down alike the small and great ! "

KING SOLOMON AND THE BEES.

FROM THE SANSCRIT.

KING SOLOMON AND THE BEES.

FROM THE SANSCRIT.

I.

HEN Solomon was reigning in his glory,
      Unto his throne the Queen of Sheba
      came,
(So in the *Talmud* you may read the story,)
   Drawn by the magic of the monarch's fame,
To see the splendors of his court ; and bring
Some fitting tribute to the mighty king.

II.

Nor this alone ; much had her Highness heard
  What flowers of learning graced the royal speech ;
What gems of wisdom dropped with every word ;
  What wholesome lessons he was wont to teach
In pleasing proverbs ; and she wished, in sooth,
To know if Rumor spoke the simple truth.

III.

Besides, the Queen had heard (which piqued her most)
  How through the deepest riddles he could spy ;
How all the curious arts that women boast
  Were quite transparent to his piercing eye ;
And so the Queen had come — a royal guest —
To put the sage's cunning to the test.

IV.

And straight she held before the monarch's view,
  In either hand, a radiant wreath of flowers ;
The one, bedecked with every charming hue,
  Was newly culled from Nature's choicest bowers ;
The other, no less fair in every part,
Was the rare product of divinest Art.

V.

" Which is the true, and which the false ? " she said.

   Great SOLOMON was silent.   All amazed,

Each wondering courtier shook his puzzled head,

   While at the garlands long the monarch gazed,

As one who sees a miracle, and fain,

For very rapture, ne'er would speak again.

VI.

" Which is the true ? " once more the woman asked,

   Pleased at the fond amazement of the King ;

" So wise a head should not be hardly tasked,

   Most learnéd Liege, with such a trivial thing ! "

But still the sage was silent ; it was plain

A deepening doubt perplexed the royal brain.

VII.

While thus he pondered, presently he sees,

   Hard by the casement, — so the story goes, —

A little band of busy, bustling bees,

   Hunting for honey in a withered rose.

The monarch smiled, and raised his royal head ;

" Open the window ! " — that was all he said.

VIII.

The window opened at the King's command ;
   Within the rooms the eager insects flew,
And sought the flowers in SHEBA'S dexter hand !
   And so the King and all the courtiers knew
That wreath was Nature's ; and the baffled Queen
Returned to tell the wonders she had seen.

IX.

My story teaches (every tale should bear
   A fitting moral) that the wise may find
In trifles light as atoms in the air
   Some useful lesson to enrich the mind, —
Some truth designed to profit or to please, —
As Israel's king learned wisdom from the bees !

ICARUS;

OR,

THE PERIL OF BORROWED PLUMES.

ICARUS.

I.

ALL modern themes of poesy are spun so
     very fine,
   That now the most amusing muse, *c. gratia,*
       such as mine,
Is often forced to cut the thread that strings our
     recent rhymes,
And try the stronger staple of the good old classic
     times.

II.

There lived and flourished long ago, in famous Ath-
    ens-town,   -
One DÆDALUS, a carpenter of genius and renown ;
('T was he who with an *augcr* taught mechanics how
    to *bore*, —
An art which the philosophers monopolized be-
    fore.)

III.

His only son was ICARUS, a most precocious lad,
The pride of Mrs. Dædalus, the image of his dad ;
And while he yet was in his teens such progress he
    had made,
He 'd got above his father's size, and much above his
    trade.

IV.

Now DÆDALUS, the carpenter, had made a pair of
    wings,
Contrived of wood and feathers and a cunning set
    of springs,

By means of which the wearer could ascend to any
  height,
And sail about among the clouds as easy as a kite!

V.

"O father," said young ICARUS, "how I should like
  to fly!
And go like you where all is blue along the upper
  sky;
How very charming it would be above the moon to
  climb,
And scamper thro' the Zodiac, and have a high old
  time!

VI.

"O would n't it be jolly, though, — to stop at all the
  inns;
To take a luncheon at 'The Crab,' and tipple at 'The
  Twins';
And, just for fun and fancy, while careering through
  the air,
To kiss the *Virgin*, tease the *Ram*, and bait the
  biggest *Bear?*

VII.

"O father, please to let me go!" was still the urchin's
  cry ;
" I 'll be extremely careful, sir, and won't go *very* high ;
O if this little pleasure-trip you only will allow,
I promise to be back again in time to fetch the
  cow ! "

VIII.

" You 're rather young," said DÆDALUS, "to tempt
  the upper air ;
But take the wings, and mind your eye with very
  special care ;
And keep at least a thousand miles below the near-
  est star ;
Young lads, when out upon a lark, are apt to go too
  far ! "

IX.

He took the wings — that foolish boy — without the
  least dismay,
(His father stuck 'em on with wax,) and so he soared
  away ;

Up — up he rises, like a bird, and not a moment
    stops
Until he's fairly out of sight beyond the mountain-
    tops !

X.

And still he flies — away — away ; it seems the
    merest fun ;
No marvel he is getting bold, and aiming at the
    sun ;
No marvel he forgets his sire ; it is n't very odd
That one so far above the earth should think him-
    self a god !

XI.

Already, in his silly pride, he's gone too far aloft ;
The heat begins to scorch his wings ; the wax is
    waxing soft ;
Down — down he goes ! — Alas ! — next day poor
    ICARUS was found
Afloat upon the Ægean Sea, extremely damp and
    drowned !

L'ENVOI.

The moral of this mournful tale is plain enough to
    all : —

Don't get above your proper sphere, or you may
    chance to fall ;

Remember, too, that borrowed plumes are most un-
    certain things ;

And never try to scale the sky with other people's
    wings !

THE STORY OF ECHO.

THE STORY OF ECHO.

I.

A BEAUTIFUL maiden was ECHO
    As classical history tells,
    A favorite nymph of DIANA,
Who dwelt among forests and dells.

II.

Now ECHO was very loquacious,
  And though she was silly and young,
It seems that she never was weary
  Of plying her voluble tongue.

III.

And I'm sorry to say, in addition,
  Besides her impertinent clack,
She had, upon every occasion,
  A habit of answering back.

IV.

Though even the wisest of matrons
  In grave conversation was heard,
Miss ECHO forever insisted
  On having the ultimate word, —

V.

A fault so exceedingly hateful,
  That JUNO (whom ECHO betrayed
While the goddess was hearing her babble)
  Determined to punish the maid.

VI.

Said she, " In reward of your folly,
   Henceforward in vain you will try
To talk in the manner of others :
   At best, you can only *reply !* "

VII.

A terrible punishment truly
   For one of so lively a turn,
And it brought the poor maiden to ruin,
   In the way you will presently learn.

VIII.

For, meeting the handsome NARCISSUS,
   And wishing his favor to gain,
Full often she tried to address him,
   But always endeavored in vain.

IX.

And when, as it finally happened,
   He spoke to the damsel one day,
Her answer seemed only to mock him,
   And drove him in anger away.

X.

Ah! sad was the fate of poor ECHO;
    Was ever so hapless a maid?
She wasted away in her sorrow,
    Until she was wholly decayed!

XI.

But her voice is still living immortal, —
    The same you have frequently heard,
When strolling in forests or valleys,
    Repeating your ultimate word!

THE CHOICE OF KING MIDAS;

OR,

TOO MUCH OF A GOOD THING.

THE CHOICE OF KING MIDAS.

I.

IDAS, King of Phrygia, several thousand
years ago,
Was a very worthy monarch, as the classic
annals show : —
You may read 'em at your leisure, when you have a
mind to doze,
In the finest Latin verses, or in choice Hellenic prose.

II.

Now this notable old monarch, King of Phrygia, as
    aforesaid,

(Of whose royal state and character there might be
    vastly more said,)

Though he occupied a palace, kept a very open door,

And had still a ready welcome for the stranger and
    the poor.

III.

Now it chanced that old SILENUS, who, it seems, had
    lost his way,

Following BACCHUS through the forest, in the pleas-
    ant month of May, —

(Which was n't very singular, for at the present day

The followers of BACCHUS very often go astray,) —

IV.

Came at last to good King MIDAS, who received him
    in his court,

Gave him comfortable lodgings, and — to cut the mat-
    ter short —

With as much consideration treated weary old SILENUS,

As if the entertainment were for MERCURY or VENUS.

V.

Now when BACCHUS heard the story, he proceeded to
the King,

And says he, "By old SILENUS you have done the
handsome thing ;

He's my much respected tutor, who has taught me
how to read,

And I'm sure your royal kindness should receive its
proper meed ;

VI.

So I grant you full permission to select your own
reward,

Choose a gift to suit your fancy, — something worthy
of a lord ! "

" *Evæ Bacche !* " cried the monarch, " if I do not make
too bold,

Let whatever I may handle be transmuted into gold!"

VII.

MIDAS, sitting down to dinner, sees the answer to his
wish,

For the turbot on the platter turns into a golden fish !

And the bread between his fingers is no longer
    wheaten bread,

But the slice he tries to swallow is a wedge of gold
    instead !

VIII.

And the roast he takes for mutton fills his mouth with
    golden meat,

Very tempting to the vision, but extremely hard to
    eat ;

And the liquor in his goblet, very rare, select, and old,

Down the monarch's thirsty throttle runs a stream of
    liquid gold !

IX.

Quite disgusted with his dining, he betakes him to his
    bed ;

But, alas ! the golden pillow does n't rest his weary
    head ;

Nor does all the gold around him soothe the monarch's
    tender skin ;

Golden sheets, to sleepy mortals, might as well be
    sheets of tin !

X.

Now poor MIDAS, straight repenting of his rash and
    foolish choice,
Went to *Bacchus*, and assured him, in a very plaintive
    voice,
That his golden gift was working in a manner most
    unpleasant ;
And the god, in sheer compassion, took away the fatal
    present.

MORAL.

By this mythologic story we are very plainly told,
That, though gold may have its uses, there are better
    things than gold ;
That a man may sell his freedom to procure the shin-
    ing pelf:
And that Avarice, though it prosper, still contrives to
    cheat itself !

THE SNAKE IN THE GLASS.

A HOMILY.

THE SNAKE IN THE GLASS.

A HOMILY.

COME listen awhile to me, my lad :
 Come listen to me for a spell ;
  Let that terrible drum
  For a moment be dumb,
For your uncle is going to tell
   What befell
A youth who loved liquor too well.

A clever young man was he, my lad ;
And with beauty uncommonly blest,
 Ere, with brandy and wine,
 He began to decline,
And behaved like a person possessed ;
  I protest
The temperance plan is the best.

One evening he went to a tavern, my lad ;
He went to a tavern one night,
 And drinking too much
 Rum, brandy, and such,
The chap got exceedingly " tight,"
  And was quite
What your aunt would entitle a " fright."

The fellow fell into a snooze, my lad ;
'T is a horrible slumber he takes ;
 He trembles with fear,
 And acts very queer ;
My eyes ! how he shivers and shakes
  When he wakes,
And raves about horrid great snakes !

'T is a warning to you and to me, my lad, —
A particular caution to all, —
    Though no one can see
    The vipers but he, —
To hear the poor lunatic bawl :
      " How they crawl ! —
All over the floor and the wall ! "

Next morning he took to his bed, my lad ;
Next morning he took to his bed ;
    And he never got up
    To dine or to sup,
Though properly physicked and bled ;
      And I read,
Next day, the poor fellow was dead !

You 've heard of the snake in the grass, my lad :
Of the viper concealed in the grass ;
    But now, you must know,
    Man's deadliest foe
Is a snake of a different class ;
      Alas ! —
'T is the viper that lurks in the glass !

A warning to you and to me, my lad ;
A very imperative call : —
>   Of liquor keep clear ;
>   Don't drink even beer,
If you 'd shun all occasion to fall ;
>   If at all,
Pray take it uncommonly small.

And if you are partial to snakes, my lad,
(A passion I think rather low,)
>   Don 't enter, to see 'em,
>   The *Devil's Museum !* —
'T is very much better to go,
>   (That's so !)
And visit a regular show.

www.ingramcontent.com/pod-product-compliance
Lightning Source LLC
Chambersburg PA
CBHW031107020726
47495CB00007B/2080